Oh Dear!

Rod Campbell

FOUR WINDS PRESS

New York

Buster went to visit
Grandma on the farm.

Grandma asked Buster
to find the eggs.

Buster went to the barn
and asked the . . .

Moo! No eggs here!
Oh dear!

So he went to the sty
and asked the . . .

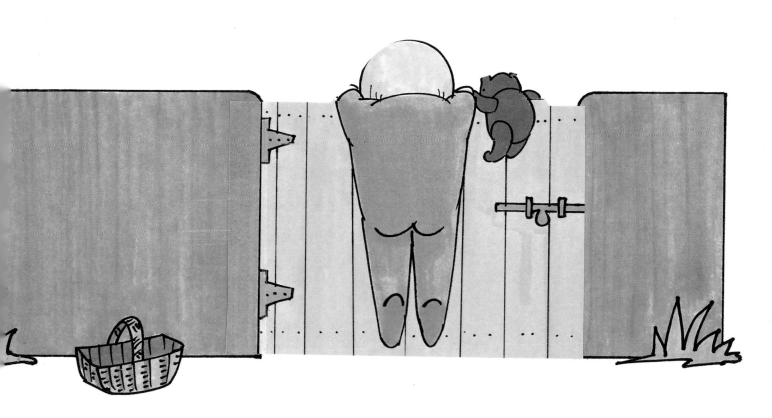

No eggs here!
Oh dear!

So he went to the field
and asked the . . .

No eggs here!
Oh dear!

So he went to the stable
and asked the . . .

No eggs here!
Oh dear!

So he went to the kennel
and asked the . . .

No eggs here!
Oh dear!

So he went to the hutch
and asked the . . .

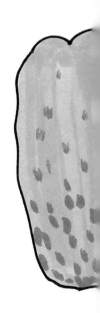

No eggs here!
Oh dear!

So he went to the pond
and asked the . . .

No eggs here!
Oh dear!

Then Buster saw
the henhouse!
So he went to the henhouse
and asked the . . .

Cluck! Lift me up!
Hooray!

For Christian and Clara

First published 1983 by Blackie and Son Ltd.
First American edition 1984 by Four Winds Press

ISBN 0-590-07944-1

Published by Four Winds Press,
a division of Scholastic Inc., 730 Broadway, New York, NY 10003

Library of Congress Catalog Card Number 84-3993

Printed and bound in Singapore